ACADIA

To my dad,
for making the parks a part
of my home

A
atheneum

ATHENEUM BOOKS FOR YOUNG READERS

An imprint of Simon & Schuster Children's Publishing Division · 1230 Avenue of the Americas, New York, New York 10020
Copyright © 2019 by Evan Turk · All rights reserved, including the right of reproduction in whole or in part in any form.
ATHENEUM BOOKS FOR YOUNG READERS is a registered trademark of Simon & Schuster, Inc.
Atheneum logo is a trademark of Simon & Schuster, Inc.
For information about special discounts for bulk purchases, please contact Simon & Schuster Special Sales
at 1-866-506-1949 or business@simonandschuster.com.
The Simon & Schuster Speakers Bureau can bring authors to your live event. For more information
or to book an event, contact the Simon & Schuster Speakers Bureau at 1-866-248-3049 or visit our
website at www.simonspeakers.com.
Book design by Ann Bobco · The text for this book was set in Requiem Text.
The illustrations for this book were rendered in pastel on black paper.
Manufactured in China · 0319 SCP · First Edition
2 4 6 8 10 9 7 5 3 1
CIP data for this book is available from the Library of Congress.
ISBN 978-1-5344-3282-6
ISBN 978-1-5344-3283-3 (eBook)

SHENANDOAH

EVAN TURK

YOU ARE HOME

An Ode to the National Parks

atheneum
ATHENEUM BOOKS FOR YOUNG READERS
New York London Toronto Sydney New Delhi

SHENANDOAH

To the chipmunk in her burrow,
sleeping beneath the leaves to keep warm;

to the resilient bison in the steaming oases
of an endless winter:

you are home.

Yellowstone

Great Sand Dunes

to the wildflowers
painting the
warming hillsides;

to the pronghorn
chewing the grass
of her first spring:
you are home.

to the prowling bobcat
slinking between slivers
of light and shadow;

Yosemite

to the constellations of blinking fireflies
in the warm summer nights:
you are home.

to the herds of elk
trumpeting the arrival of fall;

to the forests of twinkling aspen
turned golden by the shortening days:

you are home.

Rocky Mountain

to the child in the city,
surrounded by windows,
noise, and crowds;

to the child on the farm,
surrounded by endless fields;

you are home.

ZION

to the child whose
family has just
left its first footprints
on new shores;

BIG BEND

to the child whose ancestors
lived on these lands before
the stars and stripes
took them as their own:

you are still home.

MESA VERDE

beneath the
soaring doorways
of stone,

and peaks
that pierce the ceiling
of clouds;

HALEAKALĀ

within the
corridors
of ancient,
breathing
trunks
of trees,

SEQUOIA

and the teeming reefs
of the ocean floor:

you are home.

gazing toward
the highest of branches,
stretched up to the galaxies
swirling beyond the moon:

you are home.

home is a memory
of footsteps and wingbeats,
of sunrise and sunset,

GLACIER

of the moving of mountains
and rivers of ice,

GRAND CANYON

a memory carried
    through wind and rain,
echoing in canyons
    carved way down deep
    in the heart of the earth,
        and in our hearts alike.

through rising seas
and thawing ice.

a home's walls may topple,
its floors might crack,

but what keeps a home standing
can never be broken:

GRAND TETON

a sense of belonging,
sung by the streams,
from valleys to peaks,
over thousands of miles,
through millions of hearts.

from every river, star, and stone
comes the eternal refrain:

YOSEMITE

you are home.

My connection to the National Parks goes back to my childhood. My dad has been a Park Service employee for more than forty years, so my parents would take my brother and me on trips to see the most incredible places in the country. To this day, I have such vivid memories of experiences in those parks, and so many people I've talked to across the country have similarly poignant memories of National Parks that they will always cherish. I made this book to try to share the essence of being in a National Park, where the beauty, the monumental history, and the togetherness with loved ones and nature combine to leave indelible marks on our hearts.

My dad and me in Arches in 1991

Yosemite Falls

When the National Parks were first created, there had never been anything like them in the world. Some of the most miraculous areas of the country were set aside to be preserved for public use, rather than private ownership. They were designed to be places for all citizens. The parks have been called "America's Best Idea," but actually they represent both the best and the worst of this country's history. Most of these locations were home to many overlapping Native American nations, and many were and continue to be sacred places. To create the parks, thousands of people were forcibly and violently removed from their homelands or coerced into selling them to the US government. Some were banned from ever returning. Despite being "a place for all," all were not always welcome. I wanted this book to speak not just to those who already love the parks, but to anyone who has felt that "for all" didn't include them.

While the parks were officially created by wealthy and powerful white men in government, they are a testament to the work of many others as well. They are a testament to the Native Americans, who for hundreds—sometimes thousands—of years farmed, harvested, and shaped the landscapes that we now think of as wilderness. They are a testament to the Chinese immigrants and African American Buffalo Soldiers who built the roads within many of the western parks. They are a testament to the women who banded together to save the redwoods of California. They are a testament to the countless individuals and groups that saw and loved these places and wanted to make sure they were still here for future generations.

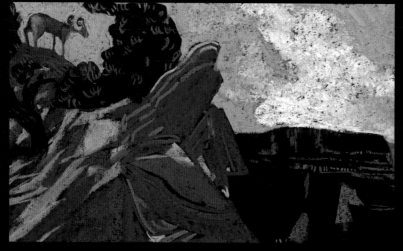

Bighorn sheep in Grand Canyon

Going forward, the parks have the chance to continue being a symbol of our country's best ideals. The United States as it exists today would likely be unrecognizable to those who set aside these lands for protection. The National Parks are now under threat from so many pressures—pollution, climate

The tallest trees in the world in Redwood

change, and politics. The parks protect vast areas of the country that surely would have been developed and exploited. They sometimes protect an entire plant or animal species, and preserve natural migration routes. Special places that could very well be National Parks, such as National Monuments and National Forests, are at an even greater risk because they do not have the protections afforded by being designated a National Park. Many of the parks now work in cooperation with local Native American nations and indigenous peoples. There is still much work to do, but the recent restoration of tribal rights to harvest in parks is a small step. Collaborative projects such as the Huna Tribal House in Glacier Bay, Kipahulu Ohana in Haleakalā National Park, and interpretive programs that allow indigenous peoples to tell their own stories help strengthen the bonds between the lands of the parks and the living cultures that are so deeply connected to them.

Within their borders, the National Parks do not just protect land, trees, or animals. They do not just protect the powerful histories that shaped them. They protect the idea of a United States that can grow to become better than its beginnings; to become inclusive of all of the nation's history and diversity. They protect spaces where the most valuable seeds of this country's future can be sown for its next generations. They preserve the limitless potential of the countless astronomers, geologists, poets, artists, athletes, and people of all kinds who come to feel the power of the places we all call home, and that is worth protecting.

ABOUT THE ART

There is nothing quite like the experience of being in one of the National Parks, so I wanted to go and draw in the parks to help bring that experience into the book. Many of the illustrations in this book were drawn on location in the National Parks, and almost all of them were based on drawings made in each of the twenty parks that I visited. The illustrations in this book were all done in pastel on black paper that I carried with me while hiking through and exploring the parks. Drawing is one of the best ways I can think of to see a National Park. There were so many times when I would be in one place drawing for a while, and the animals would come by as if I were just part of the scenery! I met chipmunks, alligators, deer, bighorn sheep, a coyote, a fox, and even a herd of bison (from the safety of a car) while drawing. If you do go out drawing in nature, always make sure someone else knows where you are, always be aware of your surroundings, and never approach a wild animal, even if it seems gentle.

Me drawing in Arches in 2018

NATIONAL PARKS OF THE UNITED STATES

MAINE

ACADIA

VERMONT

NEW HAMPSHIRE

NEW YORK

MASSACHUSETTS
CONNECTICUT
RHODE ISLAND

MICHIGAN

CUYAHOGA VALLEY

PENNSYLVANIA

NEW JERSEY

OHIO

DELAWARE

INDIANA

WEST VIRGINIA

MARYLAND

SHENANDOAH

VIRGINIA

KENTUCKY

MAMMOTH CAVE

NORTH CAROLINA

GREAT SMOKY MOUNTAINS

TENNESSEE

SOUTH CAROLINA

CONGAREE

SSISSIPPI

ALABAMA

GEORGIA

VIRGIN ISLANDS

ST. JOHN,
U.S. VIRGIN ISLANDS

FLORIDA

AMERICAN SAMOA

EVERGLADES

BISCAYNE

DRY TORTUGAS

PARKS SHOWN IN THIS BOOK

SEQUOIA,
CALIFORNIA

ZION, UTAH

GLACIER, MONTANA

ACADIA, MAINE

BIG BEND, TEXAS

GRAND CANYON,
ARIZONA

SHENANDOAH,
VIRGINIA

MESA VERDE,
COLORADO

GLACIER BAY,
ALASKA

ARCHES, UTAH

VOLCANOES, HAWAI'I

YELLOWSTONE, WYOMING/
IDAHO/MONTANA

HALEAKALĀ
HAWAI'I

GRAND TETON,
WYOMING

GREAT SAND DUNES,
COLORADO

SEQUOIA,
CALIFORNIA

GREAT SMOKY MOUNTAINS,
NORTH CAROLINA/
TENNESSEE

YOSEMITE, CALIFORNIA

BISCAYNE,
FLORIDA

YOSEMITE, CALIFORNIA

GREAT SMOKY MOUNTAINS,
NORTH CAROLINA/TENNESSEE

REDWOOD, CALIFORNIA

ROCKY MOUNTAIN,
COLORADO

EVERGLADES,
FLORIDA

OLYMPIC,
WASHINGTON

MORE ABOUT THE PARKS AND ANIMALS IN THIS BOOK

Yellowstone, Idaho/Montana/Wyoming

The first National Park in the country, and possibly the world, Yellowstone National Park was created to preserve the geothermal wonders such as geysers, steaming rocks and rivers, and mineral pools that occur on top of Yellowstone's enormous supervolcano. The park area was an important and sacred place to twenty-six different Native American nations, including the Tukudeka Shoshone who lived there year round. The US government forcibly removed them from the land in the late 1800s, ignoring signed treaties, to make way for the park. Today wildlife is abundant in the park, including black and grizzly bears, coyotes, bald eagles, elk, bighorn sheep, pronghorn, and rebounding populations of bison (or buffalo) and wolves. Bison, the largest land animals in the Americas by weight (males can weigh up to 2,000 pounds!), can also be seen in the following parks: Grand Teton, Wind Cave, Badlands, and Theodore Roosevelt.

Great Smoky Mountains, North Carolina/Tennessee

The Great Smoky Mountains are home to beautiful vistas, mountains, rivers, and wildlife. They are also home to nineteen species of fireflies, and every summer, for two weeks, you can go see their synchronous mating display. After dark, thousands of fireflies blink like silent fireworks in a magical display that draws hundreds of visitors each night. The Great Smoky area is also the homeland of the Cherokee people, but the federal government removed nearly all of them to Indian Territory on what became known as the Trail of Tears. Rounded up into stockades and forced to march west in terrible conditions, thousands of Cherokee died, especially children and elders. The few Cherokee who remained behind live on the Qualla Boundary reservation that borders the park, welcomes visitors, and includes many attractions for tourists as well as museums dedicated to Cherokee culture.

Big Bend, Texas

In south Texas, the southern border of Big Bend National Park lies along the Rio Grande, the river that divides Mexico from the United States. Encompassing enormous canyons, the Chihuahuan Desert, and the Chisos Mountains, there is an abundant variety of scenery and wildlife. Originally, the park was intended to be a joint operation, an international peace park with what are now Mexico's Maderas del Carmen and Cañón de Santa Elena Protected Natural Areas. The Chisos people made their home here for thousands of years, and in the 1700s it was inhabited and fought over by Apache, Kiowa, Comanche, and Spanish people. The federal government fought and removed the Spanish and the Native people from the area through the late 1800s to make way for American settlers. Far from any major cities, Big Bend is the darkest National Park in the contiguous United States, and offers astonishing stargazing and opportunities to see the Milky Way.

Mesa Verde, Colorado

This park preserves impressive cliff-dwelling settlements, petroglyphs, and other archaeological sites of the Ancestral Puebloan people created from 550 to 1300 AD. Nestled among sheer cliff faces, some of the villages have between fifty and two hundred rooms. Twenty-six different pueblos and tribes across the Southwest descend from the Ancestral Puebloan people. One of the nearest tribal nations, the Ute Mountain Ute Tribe, conducts Ute-led tours of similar dwellings on their own reservation near the park. The land of the National Park was originally owned by the Ute, but through a series of dishonest treaties on the part of the US government,

the tribe was forced to give up their rights to the land. This park is also a UNESCO World Heritage Site, and was the first National Park set aside in the United States to protect a man-made site.

Glacier, Montana

At the edge of the Canadian border, Glacier National Park and Waterton Lakes National Park are jointly the world's first International Peace Park. The park was carved into miraculous forms by ancient glaciers, most of which have vanished due to climate change, leaving behind turquoise glacial lakes. The park is home to a diverse array of wildlife, including mountain goats, grizzly bears, moose, mountain lions, bald eagles, bighorn sheep, and bobcats. This area was home to the Salish and Kootenai, Shoshone, Cheyenne, and most recently, the Blackfeet. It is considered a sacred place to many Native American nations. The land that became the park was reportedly sold to the United States while reserving hunting and gathering rights, but the terms of the treaty are still disputed by the Blackfeet Nation.

• • •

Bobcat

The bobcat in this book was seen in California's Yosemite National Park, but bobcats can be found across the country. You just have to look very carefully! They can also be seen in the following parks: Yellowstone, Mount Rainier, Badlands, Big Bend, Death Valley, Rocky Mountain, Great Smoky Mountains, Shenandoah, Grand Teton, and Glacier.

Elk

Elk, or *wapiti* in the Algonquin language, can be seen across the mountainous west of the country. The antlers of bull elk can reach nearly four feet in length! They travel in herds and are one of the largest land animals in the area after the bison and moose. The elk in this book were seen in Rocky Mountain National Park in Colorado, but they can also be seen in the following parks: Yellowstone, Grand Teton, Redwood, Glacier, and even the Great Smoky Mountains, where a herd was recently reintroduced.

Grizzly Bear

Also known as the North American brown bear, these giants can weigh up to eight hundred pounds. The bear family in this book was depicted in Grand Teton National Park in Wyoming, but they can also be seen in the following parks: Yellowstone, Glacier, Katmai, Denali, Glacier Bay, and Kenai Fjords.

Pronghorn

Although they look like antelope, pronghorn are actually more closely related to giraffes. They are one of the fastest land animals in the world, and possibly evolved to escape a now-extinct prehistoric American cheetah. These pronghorn were depicted in Great Sand Dunes National Park in Colorado, but they can also be seen in the following parks: Yellowstone, Grand Teton, Wind Cave, Badlands, and Theodore Roosevelt.